this VeggieTales® gift book belongs to:

Jackson + Samuel

Grandmommie + PawPa
from

Oct. 11, 2007
date

Published by Howard Publishing Co., Inc.
3117 North 7th Street, West Monroe, Louisiana 71291-2227
www.howardpublishing.com

06 07 08 09 10 11 12 13 14 15   10 9 8 7 6 5 4 3 2 1

Photography by Chrys Howard and LinDee Loveland © Howard Publishing Co., Inc.

ISBN 1-58229-480-1 (Stand Up!)

Stand! Words and Music by Phil Vischer and Kurt Heinecke.
© 1995 Bob & Larry Publishing (ASCAP)

I Can Be Your Friend reminds us that friends come in all shapes and sizes. If we'll just look beyond what we see on the outside, we'll find the treasure of new friends everywhere.

In *My Day*, Junior shares about his day through prayer as children learn how to develop their own prayer relationship with God.

Based on the best-loved Silly Song with Larry, *Oh, Where Is My Hairbrush?* is sure to delight every VeggieTales® fan.

God Is Bigger! is a fun way to remind children that God is always near and strong enough to protect them—even from the boogie man.

A thankful heart truly is a happy heart! This fun book instills the value of gratitude and demonstrates how to express thankfulness to those who love us.

CD of accompanying VeggieTales® song included with each book!

Stand Up!

written by Phil Vischer
illustrated by Casey Jones and John Trent

BIG IDEA BOOKS

HOWARD
PUBLISHING CO

When friends are pushing us to do what's wrong,
it's not always easy to stand up
for what we believe in.
But with God standing with us
and our parents standing behind us,
we can make choices that will
make them very proud.

Sing along with the enclosed CD
as you read the words and enjoy
the pictures that bring this
special song to life!

My mommy always taught me to do what's right,

That's why she tells me
what I need to know!

But sometimes when I'm playin' with a buddy or two,

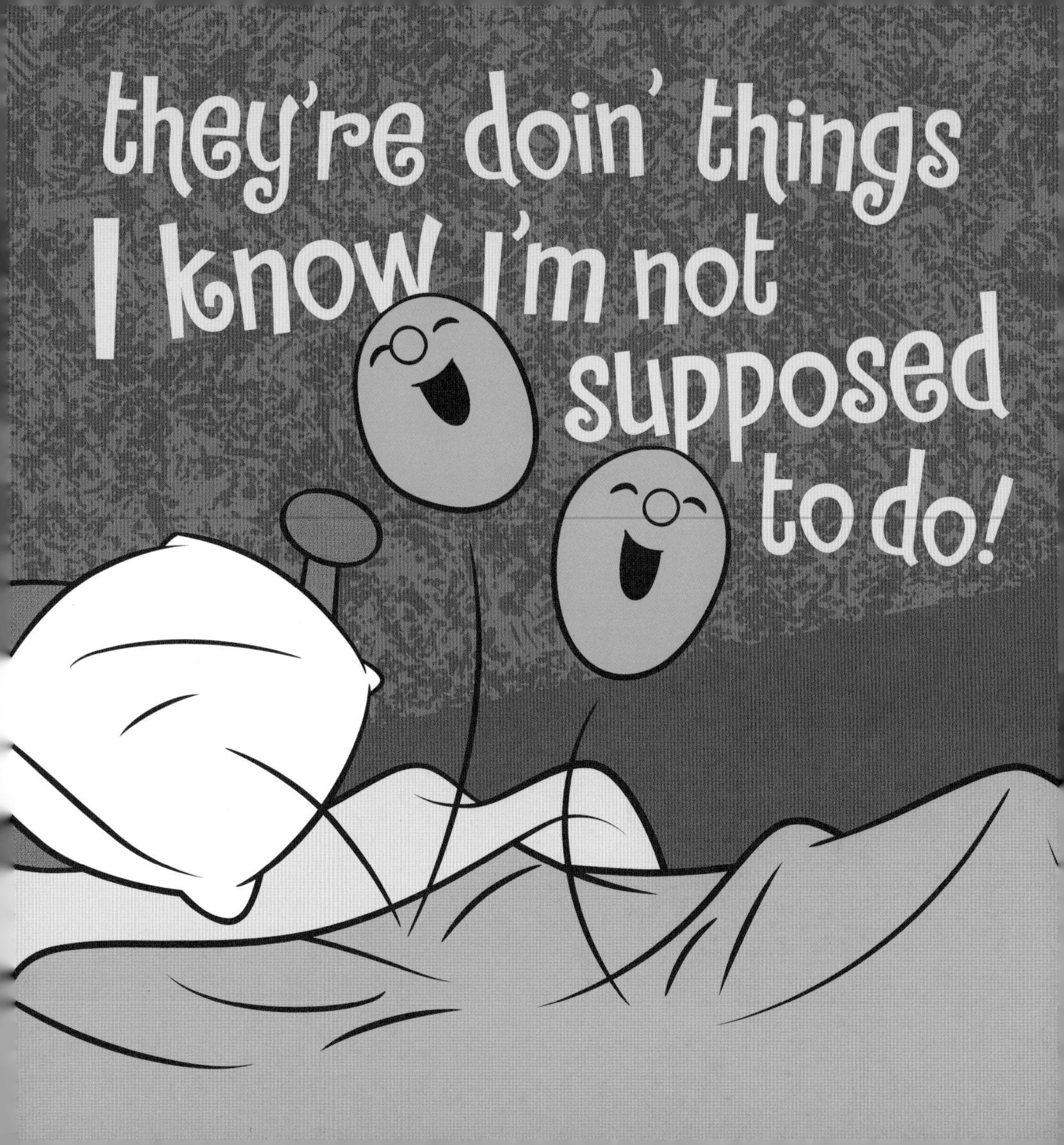
they're doin' things
I know I'm not
supposed
to do!

even though the things they do are wrong?

Hmm-mmm! I remember, "STAND!"

Stand up! Stand up!

for what you believe in, believe in. Believe, and God...

He's the one to back you up!

...will stand with you!

When everybody tells ya that ya gotta be cool,

remember what you learned in church and Sunday school!

just check it out.
The Bible
tells us
what it's
all about!

and he can tell you if a thing is good or bad.

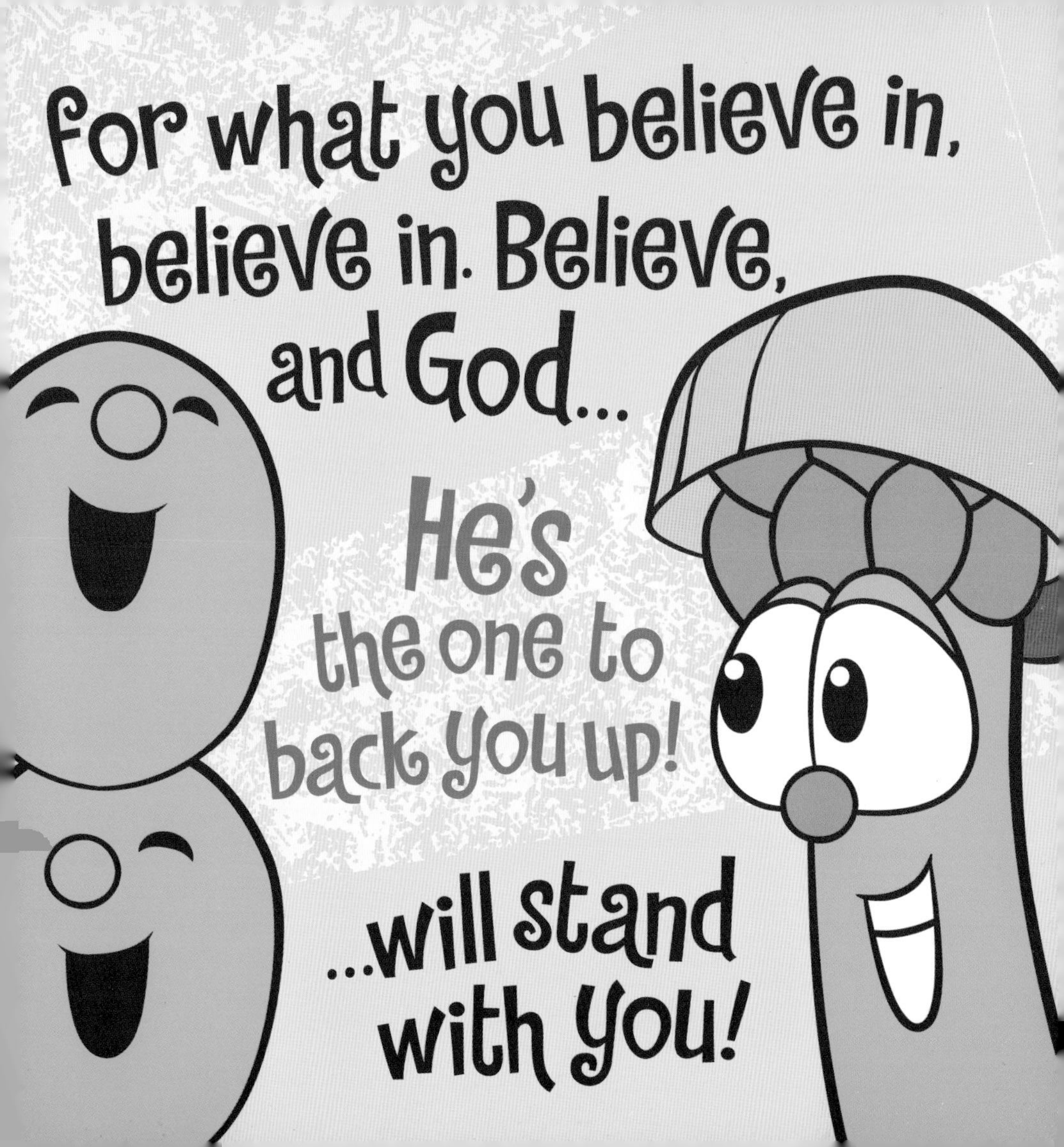

For what you believe in,
believe in. Believe, and God...

He's the one
to back you up!

...will stand
with you!

He'll stand
with you!